Pop Bottles

Also by Ken Roberts

Crazy Ideas

Pop Bottles

Ken Roberts

A Groundwood Book
Douglas & McIntyre
Vancouver/Toronto

Douglas & McIntyre Limited
1615 Venables Street
Vancouver, British Columbia

Canadian Cataloguing in Publication Data

Roberts, Ken, 1946–
    Pop bottles

ISBN 0-88899-059-6

I. Title.

PS8585.023P66 1987   jC813'.54   C87-093341-8
PZ7.R62Po 1987

Cover art by Graham Bardell
Design by Michael Solomon
Printed and bound in Canada by D.W. Friesen & Sons Ltd.

To

J. Westerby,
who watched the story change.

Acknowledgements

I would like to thank my father, Mr. W.F. Roberts, and Cliff Shoop of Nanaimo for stories of their youths. My father really did live in a house with a pop-bottle walkway, and Mr. Shoop often wore an outfit similar to Ray's.

I would also like to thank Lynn Shoop, Jeremy Roberts, Cara Roberts, the Grocery Hall of Fame in Vancouver, the Richmond Public Library and the Vancouver Public Library.

Incredible as it may seem, the quirk of fate that determines the final bolo-bat contest actually happened to my father when he was a boy.

ONE SUMMER DAY
1933

One

Will stood in his front yard, playing with his bolo-bat. A bolo-bat is a simple contraption. A wooden paddle is attached to a piece of elastic, and the elastic is connected to a red rubber ball.

Will hit the ball, waited for it to speed out and race back, and then hit it again. Over and over. Will was trying hard to become the best bolo-bat paddler in the world. He had plenty of time to practise. Will's bolo-bat was the only toy he owned.

While he batted, Will could hear his dad's rocking chair squeaking. His dad sat on the porch and stared at mountains almost as much as Will practised the bolo-bat. Neither one of them had much else to do.

Early each morning Will's dad, like most adults in the neighbourhood, left home and waited in line down at some factory or mill, hoping for a day's work. Sometimes he would get lucky and there would be a small job. Most of the time he was home before Will woke up, sitting on the porch and watching the mountain shadows change with the early morning light. Will's dad thought a lot while he looked at mountains.

Will did his thinking while he paddled. It wasn't thinking like wondering how the ancient Egyptians had built pyramids. It was the kind of thinking that usually got him in trouble. On this summer morning Will figured out something that was going to cause more trouble than anything he'd ever thought of before. Will actually missed his red ball when the idea hit. He didn't care much about the missing. His mind was caught.

Will wrapped the bolo-bat string around his paddle and stared at his dad. He climbed the steps to the porch, looked up at the mountains and decided to test his idea.

"Those mountains sure look pretty, Dad."

His dad sighed. "Sure do."

Will reached into his pocket and pulled out a rock.

"I found this rock today. It sure is pretty, too."

His dad didn't even glance at the rock.

"Sure is," he said without the sigh.

Will stuffed the rock into his pocket and grinned.

"I'll be back in a while, Dad," he said, racing down the steps. "See you later!"

Will's dad didn't answer. He just kept staring and rocking.

Will ran the whole two blocks to Ray Fanthorpe's house, his bare feet smacking against the concrete sidewalk. There were a lot of cracks and rocks to avoid. The City of Vancouver hadn't placed much importance on sidewalks since the Depression hit. Nobody, not even the city, had money to spend.

"Ray! Ray!" Will yelled from half a block away. He could see Ray hunched under a tree, trying to stay in a small patch of mid-day shade. Ray always seemed to be hiding from the sun. His clothes were the problem. Even on scorching hot days Ray wore the same outfit — long pants, a wool sweater and shiny black shoes. Every other kid Will knew wore cut-offs and hand-me-down shirts. Ray dressed like every day was Easter.

Ray jumped up and motioned for Will to stay quiet. He shielded his eyes from the sun and ran up the steps to his house, disappearing inside.

Ray's parents didn't like Will. Will had never even seen the inside of his best friend's home.

The screen door squeaked open and Ray hurried out. He glanced over his shoulder to make sure his parents weren't looking.

"Hi, Will. Let's scoot around the corner."

"Ray," said Will excitedly, "I just figured out something."

"What?"

"It's about adults. Guess what? They only notice big things. They never look at anything small."

"What?"

"Think about it. When we're at the beach adults stare out at the ocean and admire the sunset. Kids dig in the sand and look for shells. My dad stares at mountains all day. I hit a little red ball."

"So?"

"Kids own the ground, Ray! We can find things adults can't."

"I don't get it."

"Okay. Here's an experiment. Look down and tell me what you see."

Ray looked down.

"Well?"

"Dog poop."

Will looked down, too. "Yeah, but there's a shoe print in it, a big print. Some adult stepped in that dog poop."

"So?"

"So the adult didn't notice it, and we did." Will slid past on tiptoes. "Keep looking."

"I see two ants," said Ray, "and a weed. A gum wrapper. And a penny. A penny!" Ray reached down and picked it up.

Will grinned. "Fifteen adults probably walked past that penny, but it took a kid to find it. We should go someplace where there's lots of adults, Ray, rich adults. Someplace where they might be reaching into their pockets. Maybe a parking lot. I'll bet a lot of people spill change when they pull out their car keys. We'll get rich. Hey! I just thought of something else.''

''What?''

''We can pretend to be older by saying things like, 'Beautiful sunset yesterday.' ''

''What do you mean, Will?''

''You know, if we want to stay out late or want girls to think we're older.''

''Everyone knows we're twelve.''

''Yeah, but they'll think we're more mature if we admire big stuff like scenery.''

Ray stopped and scratched his chin. ''I think you're right.''

''I know I am,'' said Will. ''Adults look up . . .'' Will looked up, spread his arms, breathed deeply and tried to look like he really did admire clouds in the sky. '' . . . and kids look down.'' Will looked down, his eyes searching the ground. They came to rest on a weed-infested walkway leading up to an abandoned house. The path was made from thousands of dark smooth circles arranged in rows. It was an odd-looking pathway.

Will saw lots of odd things every day, and they didn't usually bother him. He didn't stop to inspect them or think about them for longer than a second or two. But when his eyes reached those small circles, one of them caught the sun and shone up, like a beckoning star.

Will opened a gate and kicked at one ring, his bare foot skimming against something hard and smooth. He stood still for a moment.

"What are you doing?" asked Ray.

Will didn't even hear him. He quickly dropped to his knees, pushed aside a couple of weeds and dusted off one of the small round circles. It was the bottom of a pop bottle. Next to it was another pop bottle and next to that another. The bottles had been buried upside down so that only the glassy bottoms poked up through the dirt. Somebody, years before, had made a walkway from thousands of pop bottles. Stores paid two cents each for empty pop bottles.

Will gulped. His hands began to sweat. He leaned over until one eye almost touched a bottle, and he peered down inside. He could see the whole bottle. It wasn't cracked or chipped.

Buried in that walkway was more money than most families made in a month.

"Hug a walnut!" shouted Will, leaping up.

"What's that mean, 'Hug a walnut?' " asked Ray. "You say it a lot."

"It means I'm excited," said Will, leaping around and making silly faces.

But why say 'Hut a walnut?'' Why not 'Gosh, I'm excited?' ''

"Ray! Forget about 'Hug a walnut' and just take a good look at this walkway.''

Ray stared at the circles of glass.

"Closer,'' said Will.

"What?''

"Look closer.''

"How much closer?''

"Get down here.''

"This better be worth it,'' said Ray as he squatted next to the path, being careful not to touch his pants on the ground or scuff his shoes. He moved a couple of weeds with a handkerchief so his hands wouldn't get dirty.

"There're all bottles,'' said Ray, surprised.

"Pop bottles,'' corrected Will.

"They aren't chipped or anything, are they?''

"I can see right down inside one of them. It's fine.''

"Then they're a treasure,'' said Ray breathlessly.

"Right.''

"What's a treasure?'' asked a deep voice. Ray stood up. He and Will slowly turned around.

"Hi, creeps.''

It was Marty Robinson. Marty was fifteen, and he thought the neighbourhood was his official kingdom.

There had never been any revolutions. Marty Robinson was huge, and mean.

"What?" asked Will innocently.

"I said, what's a treasure? You tell me, Ray Fanthorpe. If you don't, I'll mess up your hair, scuff your shoe polish and pull that sweater over your head. Out with it. What treasure? Why were you two kneeling down there?"

Ray hunched over to protect his sweater. He turned in the toes of his shoes so they wouldn't stick out.

"We weren't talking about real treasure," muttered Will. "We're just little kids, right? We were playing a game."

Marty frowned. Will could see each mental gear shift slowly into place.

"Then why's Fanthorpe so jumpy?" Marty asked at last.

"Why? You ask why? Just last week you chased him five long blocks for not moving over when you came waddling down the sidewalk."

"Hey, that's right. I did!"

Ray looked at Will and winced. Will shrugged. He had to do something to distract Marty Robinson.

"Never did catch him, either," muttered Marty, wheels turning. Marty Robinson never forgot anything. He was like a giant elephant. It just took a while for memories to travel to all parts of his body.

8

Ray took off down the sidewalk. He ran flat footed so he wouldn't hurt the shine on his shoes. He didn't run as fast as he could. Fanthorpes didn't sweat unless it was absolutely necessary, and it wasn't just then. Marty Robinson's absence of speed and slowness of memory were all that kept neighbourhood kids from becoming extinct.

"He's getting away," said Will calmly.

"Getting away?" repeated Marty, suddenly alert.

Will grinned as Marty barrelled down the street. Ray would understand, of course, why he'd had to trick Marty Robinson into forgetting about treasure and sidewalks. It would be worth a chase if it kept Marty from noticing those bottles. Will took another look at the pathway and checked the address — 374 West 14th. He pulled out his bolo-bat and began to paddle as he slowly ambled home.

LATER

Two

Will stopped in front of his house. His dad was still sitting on the porch, staring at mountains. Will sat on the bottom step. It squeaked a little.

"Saw a good play yesterday," said Mr. McCleary without taking his eyes off Hemlock Mountain. "You'd like it. There's a lot of silly misunderstanding and running around. I'll take you Monday night if you want. Different ushers."

Will's dad loved plays, but he couldn't afford tickets. When he really wanted to go, he'd put on a worn-out suit jacket, walk to the theatre and wait. People poured out during intermission, seeking fresh air. Jim McCleary would mingle with them and walk back inside. He'd find an empty seat and watch the second half free. Jim McCleary had seen the endings of hundreds of plays and was an expert at piecing together half-told tales. Still, he never invited Will to go with him unless . . .

"Dad?"

"Yeah?"

"Where's Mom?"

"Down at the church teaching piano, I suppose."

"Dad?"

"Yeah?"

"When are we moving?"

Will asked it just like that, direct and sudden, to see if he could get his dad to take his eyes off those mountains. It was a secret contest of his. He didn't win this time.

"Tomorrow," said Jim McCleary.

There was no need to ask why. The McClearys moved every three months, four at most, even when the house they were staying in had a perfect view of the mountains and the rent was low. They moved because of Will's mom.

Anna McCleary was a nomad. Her parents had been missionaries, and she had been born in the desert somewhere in southern Russia. When she was eleven years old Anna's parents decided to move back to Canada. Anna didn't want to go, but it was 1913 and there were rumours of war. They left with traders and travelled unknown mountain passes to Istanbul. From there they sailed to Halifax and rode by car to the family farm near Springhill, Nova Scotia. It was Anna's first car ride. She loved it so much that she almost forgot about the desert.

Anna spent that summer on the farm, begging for rides in the Model T. In the fall she went away to school. Anna was a good student, although she did find it impossible to settle into one bed and one room. She was a nomad and had to keep moving.

When she grew up, nomad instincts made Anna McCleary a happy person during Depression years. She never wanted to accumulate more than she and her family could cram into boxes with an hour's notice. She was a smiler, and she lifted the spirits of everyone she knew. She just liked to move a lot.

"Are we moving far?" asked Will.

"Nope. Just five blocks. It's an old repossessed house. Been empty for awhile."

"What's the address?"

"374 West 14th."

At that moment, if Jim McCleary had glanced at his son for even a second, he would have seen a bug-eyed, open-mouthed face. He probably would have jumped off the porch, grabbed Will and started running for the hospital. There was nothing wrong with Will, though, except a touch of shock.

Thousands and thousands of pop bottles. Buried treasure. And now he, Will McCleary, age twelve, was going to live with them and walk on them and . . .

"Do you mind moving again, Will?"

"No, Dad. This move is just fine."

Three

Five of Will's friends, besides Ray, stood in the yard. They were surrounded by boxes and bags, ready for the move. They'd come to help so they could feel rings of refund money with their toes. Will shouldn't have told them about the pop bottles, but he did. He wasn't good at keeping secrets when he was excited, unless it was keeping secrets from his parents or from Marty Robinson.

"Landsakes," said Will's mom, rubbing her hands on her skirt. "So many kids to help us move. We can't pay. You told them that, didn't you, Will?"

"They know," said Will.

"Then we'd best be going," said Anna McCleary, slinging eastern saddlebags over one shoulder and tucking a box under an arm.

Ray picked up the cleanest box he could find. His parents thought Will was moving far away. Ray had made it sound that way when he asked them if he could help. He'd put a sadness in his voice. So, his

13

parents had let him come and even let him dress in what they called rags. Ray was still, of course, the best-dressed person in the yard. He wore a sweater and his pants were pressed. There was an ink stain near one of the pockets, though.

"I couldn't borrow a car," said Jim McCleary to Will's friends. "We'll have to carry everything."

"That's all right," said Ray. "We don't mind."

"Not a wee bit!" yelled out Colin, a skinny kid from Scotland. Some days, when there was nothing else to do, Will and Colin would sit and talk, each trying to figure out what the other was saying. They'd have a good time, laughing when some word had to be spelled out in the dirt.

Everyone started nabbing boxes and walking down the street. The parade of movers meandered around a tricycle on the sidewalk and weaved past a black Model A with two flat tires in the Westerby driveway.

Will picked up the entire contents of his room, bedding under one arm, clothes in a box under the other, and spare shoes around his neck.

"We could buy the Westerby car," said Will's mom with an impish grin. "They'll sell it cheap. Fifty dollars. I've asked."

"I'm sure you have," said Will's dad.

"Oh, a car would be wonderful. I wouldn't have to move so much if we had a car. I could ride around

14

and see new places. But don't worry. I don't want a car today."

"Why?"

"Are you kidding? Look at that line of kids hauling boxes. It reminds me of a desert caravan."

Jim McCleary hugged his wife.

"Well," interrupted Will, "we'd better go. We're eating dust already."

Will's mom laughed. She was always talking about days when she'd walked at the back of the caravan, breathing in dust kicked up from shuffling feet.

Anna McCleary let out a whoop and set off after her parade of movers.

"This," she yelled back to Will and his dad, "is one caravan I want to follow. Besides, I don't think they'll kick up much dust. It's a pity we didn't have sidewalks in the desert."

Anna McCleary raced off. Will smiled as he watched her. He smiled partly because she'd mentioned sidewalks without realizing how important one short sidewalk was to him. He smiled mostly because he wouldn't trade her for any other mom in the world. How many other moms would laugh and skip because they didn't have enough money for a rented truck when they moved.

"I hope you don't mind that we're moving again," said Will's dad. "She's special, you know. I don't want to tame the nomad inside her."

"It's okay, Dad. Really."

By the time Will and his dad reached the house, the caravan had disappeared inside. There was a pile of worn shoes and socks inside the front gate.

"They . . . they left their shoes out here," said Jim McCleary, puzzled. "Now, why on earth would . . ."

"I don't know," interrupted Will, "but we'd better do the same thing. It's probably some nomad tradition Mom just remembered."

Will was wearing shoes because it was the easiest way to get them to the new house. They'd sort of moved themselves. He kicked them off, stretched out one big toe, and ran it around the rim of the nearest bottle. His dad couldn't see. He was sitting at the curb, facing the street and fiddling with a knot in one shoelace.

"I'll start in toward the house," said Will impatiently.

"Sure," answered his dad as he tackled one last knot. Will carefully stepped on top of a bottle bottom. The glass felt cool and smooth. He looked down. Some of the bottles were green. Some were a darkish brown. Others were clear. All sparkled in the sunlight.

Will peered down at a clear one. That bottle was worth two cents, and he was standing on it.

Will suddenly noticed another set of feet facing his. A couple of toes were poking at the dirt around the side of a bottle.

"Ray?" asked Will without glancing up.

"How'd you know it was me?" asked Ray.

"It's your feet," said Will, beginning to giggle. "Those are the cleanest feet I've ever seen. You must wash them every week."

"Every week! I wash them every day!"

"Anna," yelled Jim McCleary from behind Will. "How come we have to take off our shoes?"

Will's mom stood on the porch with her hands on her hips. She was laughing. Will swivelled around and stared at his dad. He was holding tattered shoes in one hand and socks in the other. His pants were rolled up. He looked like someone preparing to wade in the ocean.

"Your shoes? Landsakes, I don't know. All those kids just took theirs off when they got here."

"It wasn't your idea?"

"Course not."

Jim McCleary threw his shoes onto the sidewalk, sat down heavily beside them, and started to pull them on again. Will and Ray looked at each other and grinned.

"Where is everybody?" asked Will. "I expected to see them out here walking on bottles."

"They're in the backyard."

"Why?"

"Because," said Ray, grinning even more, "there's a huge patio back there and guess what it's made from?"

"Pop bottles?"

Ray nodded.

"Hug a walnut," said Will, and both boys sighed. In western movies old prospectors were always searching for the "mother lode" — some hidden valuable mine. Without spending years in desert mountains, Will and Ray had found themselves a genuine mother lode.

"I'm standing on twelve cents," said Ray at last. "Six cents with each foot."

"I'm standing on sixteen cents," said Will proudly. "Got big feet."

"You sure are lucky," said Ray.

"It sure feels good," agreed Will.

THE NEXT DAY

Four

Will's dad roamed the front porch, adjusting his chair in a search for the best possible mountain view. Will and Ray could hear him mutter every few minutes. He was having a hard time finding a tunnel through the trees and houses.

Will knew his dad wouldn't be leaving the porch for hours. His mom was gone, too. She was teaching piano in the church basement. She had learned to play at boarding school. The McClearys didn't own a piano. A piano was too big to move. Jim McCleary loved to kid his wife about playing such a massive instrument. He figured a nomad like her should have mastered something small, like the flute.

Since Will's parents were both busy, he and Ray were free to count the pop bottles in the backyard patio. Will did the actual counting. He didn't mind moving around on his knees. Ray sat on a wooden box and wrote down figures.

"There are enough bottles back here to pay our rent for a whole year," muttered Will as he stopped to stretch his back. "Ray?"

"Yeah?"

"You go to church more than me, don't ya?"

"Guess so. Sure."

"We haven't talked about this, but it's a sin to steal, right?"

"Course."

"I mean, my parents are just renting this place. The bank owns it. So, we can't take anything that's part of the house without it being a sin."

"That's right."

"These bottles aren't part of the house, though, are they?"

"No," said Ray, "but the bank owns the yard, too."

"Do you think the bank people know they own a walkway and a patio made from soda pop bottles?"

"Probably not, Will. But it doesn't make any difference. God knows."

"Ray?"

"Yeah?"

"Do you always have to add a 'but?' "

Ray thought for a moment. "I guess I'm being your conscience."

"You mean if I could convince you, no 'buts,' then it would be all right to cash in these bottles?"

Ray wiped dust off his shoes. He untied his laces so he could clean the leather tongue and think.

"Are you asking me to be your conscience?"

"Why not?"

"Don't you have one of your own?"

"Sure."

"And what does it say?"

"It says take the bottles."

"Then do it."

"No."

"Why not?"

"I don't think my conscience works as well as yours, Ray. It's not in shape, see. You go to church more, and you never get in trouble or anything."

"So your conscience is worried about taking these bottles?"

"Nope. I just don't trust what the thing is saying. I'm a kid."

"So am I."

Will rolled his eyes. "Believe me, Ray, you do not have the conscience of a normal twelve-year-old."

Ray picked at a piece of lint on his sweater and thought some more. The bottles weren't in his yard. It was Will who was dying to harvest them like carrots. Besides, being an honorary conscience was kind of a compliment. And his parents were always telling him that Fanthorpes were bred to exercise power.

"Okay, I'll do it. I'll be your conscience. Convince me." Ray crossed his arms and tried to look stern.

"Great!" said Will, grinning and walking on his knees over to Ray so he could stare him in the eyes. "Try this. My family's only going to live in this house for a couple of months. If I don't cash in those bottles, the next tenants probably will."

"No good," said Ray, shaking his head and holding up one hand like a policeman stopping traffic. You can't steal just because somebody else might. Besides, the bottles have been here for years. Like you said, adults don't look at the ground much."

"How about if I give a part of the money to your church? Or to a soup kitchen? We could feed a lot of people. These bottles could do a lot of good. Hardly anybody on this street has a regular job."

"Nope. That's a bribe. The money wouldn't be a gift. It'd be an excuse for you keeping most of it."

Will stood up and paced back and forth on the pop-bottle patio. He reached into his back pocket, pulled out his bolo-bat and began to smack the small red ball.

So," said Will, still paddling, "the only way I can dig up these bottles and still please you, my conscience, would be if it wasn't stealing. Right?"

"Right," repeated Ray.

"And the only way it wouldn't be stealing would be to get the bank's permission. Right?"

"But . . . nobody at any bank is going to give you those bottles."

"But if they did?" asked Will.

"It wouldn't be stealing," admitted Ray.

"Let's go, then."

"Where?"

"To the bank."

Will bounced the little red ball off his elbow and forehead before catching it with his teeth. It was his special ending. He wrapped the elastic around the paddle and shoved the bolo-bat into his back pocket.

"I'm not going," said Ray. "I'd be too embarrassed."

"You have to go," said Will, pulling on a shoe. "You're my conscience. What if I just pretend to see the manager? Or what if he says I can have the bottles? Would you believe me if you weren't there to hear it?"

Will started walking around the side of the house. Ray reached over to tie his laces. He tried to do it fast, too fast, and wound up with only one loop on his right shoe. One loop wasn't good enough for a Fanthorpe, so he pulled the knot loose and started again.

"Wait!" yelled Ray as he finished the knot and ran after Will. He caught him at the corner. "They'll never let you have those bottles. I mean, there's probably a hundred dollars in that yard.''

"We'll see," said Will, eyes forward and stride determined, just like one of the heroes he liked so much in the Saturday afternoon matinee westerns. "Just remember, whatever happens, don't say a word.''

The bank had two columns in front, like a Greek temple. The floor inside was marble, and the counters were oak. Noise echoed, like in a church. Everything was dusty and slightly tattered.

Will and Ray stood beside the door, looking at the counters and the lines of people.

"It's not like a store, is it, Will?''

"What did you expect? A sale on twenty-dollar bills?''

"Have you ever been in a bank before, Will?''

"No. Have you?''

"No. I don't see any other kids, either. Let's get out of here. I'm nervous.''

"Okay, let's go.''

"You mean it?''

"All you have to do is admit it's all right for me to take those bottles, and we'll leave.''

"Of all the nerve! Blackmailing your own conscience. You can't make deals with right and wrong!''

24

"Boys! Boys! Stop that racket," said a pear-shaped, middle-aged man in a loose-fitting suit. He flipped open a gate in the counter and walked over to them. "What are you two doing here, anyway?"

Will and Ray glanced at each other.

"We're looking for the manager," said Will in a whisper.

"That's me."

"My family and I just moved into one of your houses," said Will, glancing across at Ray.

"Yes?" asked the manager solemnly, waiting for another message about not being able to pay the rent.

"Yeah. Anyway, when we moved in, I discovered some soda pop bottles still on the property. They were buried. Since those bottles were already there, my conscience told me they rightfully belong to you, to the bank. So, I came to ask if I could have them."

"Pop bottles?"

"Yes, sir. Buried in the ground."

"And you came to ask for them?"

"Yeah. See, they're worth a couple of cents each at the grocery store."

Ray started to say something, but Will nudged him hard.

"Why, that's commendable, lad."

"What do you mean, sir?" Will asked innocently.

"It's just that most people simple would have taken the bottles."

"I thought it only fair to tell you, sir," said Will, forehead furrowed with sincerity. "After all, the bottles do belong to the bank."

"Not now, my boy," said the manager with a growing grin. "They're yours, a reward for being so honest. Go buy yourself a bit of candy."

"Hug a walnut! Thank you, sir!"

Will held out his hand. The bank manager shook it firmly and then left to whisper to the tellers and point at Will, an honest lad.

"That was easy," said Will happily, rubbing his hands together with greed as he turned to Ray. "Let's get out of here. Fast."

"But . . . but," stammered Ray, "he thinks there are only a couple of bottles. There are thousands!"

"Keep your voice down," said Will. "If he'd asked how many there were I would have told him. He didn't ask."

"But he thinks that . . ."

"I don't care what he thinks. I asked if I could have the bottles. He said yes."

"But . . ."

"No buts. He said 'yes.' The bottles are mine. Let's go."

Will walked out the door. Ray ran to catch up.

"Okay," said Ray, "legally, I suppose it's not stealing for you to cash in those bottles. But your parents are going to take them for themselves when they find out.''

''The bottles are mine. Not theirs. I found them. I asked for them. The bank manager gave them to me.''

''But when you start digging them up . . .''

''My parents won't know.''

''But when they see you . . .''

''They won't.''

''But when they see bottles missing . . .''

''I told you before, adults look up, not down.''

''Yeah, but your mom's different.''

''Don't worry so much. Meet me in front of the house at ten o'clock tonight.''

Five

Will quietly squeezed through a big hole in the screen door. It was dark outside, but some light shone through the living-room window. Will stared down at the walkway. Each bottle looked like a black hole aimed toward the centre of the earth.

"You there, Ray?" whispered Will.

Ray poked up from beside the porch. He wore good pants, his sweater and a bow tie. His hair was oiled smooth and shiny.

"Geez," said Will, "you look like you're going to meet the King or something. We're here to dig up pop bottles. Why are you dressed like that?"

"Sorry. We always dress for dinner, and I'm supposed to stay dressed for the evening. My parents think I'm out on a night-time nature project. I can't be gone long. I won't really get dirty, will I?"

"Great, Ray. We're supposed to be mining these things, you know. They don't just pop out of the ground!"

"I can't help what my parents make me wear, Will! What am I supposed to do?"

"Aw, just keep watch."

"Won't your parents notice that some of the bottles are missing?" asked Ray nervously, looking up at the house.

"Nah. I got it all worked out. See, we'll take just enough bottles so we can both go to the movies and . . ."

"Both?"

"Sure. You're here, aren't you? Even if you're not digging, you're still my partner. We'll mine enough for a bit of candy, too. And we'll give ten cents to each kid who helped us move. We have to take thirty bottles for . . ."

"Thirty! They'll notice!"

"Shh!"

"Don't say *shh*. My dad says nothing travels farther than the sound of somebody saying *shh*."

"Well, just shut up, then. Listen. Nobody's going to notice because there won't be any holes. I'm going to dig up eighty bottles and replant the extra fifty so they're spread over the same area. It'll be like thinning a vegetable patch. You take some away, but the patch is still there."

Will pulled a rusty trowel from under the porch and quickly began to shovel dirt from around a bottle.

"I thought we'd start close to the porch," said Will. "It might look like the bottles always started thin. Besides, I don't think Dad can see this part of the walkway from his mountain-staring chair."

Will started digging up bottles and brushing them off. Some he slipped under the porch. Others he stacked to be replanted.

"Ray?"

"Yeah?"

"I put some rocks over there by the corner of the house. Since we're taking bottles out of the ground, we've got to bury something else or there won't be enough dirt. Carry some rocks around here, would you?"

"Sure," whispered Ray as he crouched down and edged his way around the corner of the porch. "Duck!" said Ray suddenly.

Will left a bottle half out of the ground and scurried under the porch. Ray was already there. Will knew it must be serious. It was wet under the porch, and mud was getting on Ray's shoes. Will peeked between two of the steps. A huge shadowy lump was moving slowly along the sidewalk in front of the house. It stopped and opened the gate. The shadow dropped to the ground and pulled out a trowel. It started to dig.

"He's stealing our bottles," said Ray quietly.

"Who?"

"Marty Robinson," whispered Ray, shivering.

"He must have come back and figured out about the pop bottles."

"Let's scream," said Ray.

Will slapped a hand over Ray's mouth.

"No! We've got half the walkway dug up ourselves. And we're hiding under the steps with dirt on us. Marty'll just leave if you scream. And then who'll get in trouble?"

"Us?"

"Right."

The two boys turned and silently watched as Marty Robinson pulled out twenty bottles. When he was finished, he loped off down the sidewalk, a canvas bag perched over one shoulder.

"That swine," muttered Ray.

"It's like cattle rustling," said Will.

"We'll get even."

"Yeah. Sure. But right now we have to finish our job and then cover Marty's holes, too. If my parents see his mess they'll realize the walkway's a gold mine."

"A gold mine somebody else is trying to claim jump," snapped Ray.

Will nodded slowly.

Not even the mud oozing into Ray's shoes could make him smile.

THE NEXT MORNING

Six

Ray and Will sat under a tree, a bag of bottles between them. They weren't smiling. When Marty realized somebody was covering his trail, he'd steal more. The pop bottles were supposed to be a treasure. A treasure was like a gift. You shouldn't have to work for gifts.

"Where do we turn in our bottles?" asked Ray.

There were two candy stores close by. Both redeemed empty pop bottles. Ray's parents wouldn't let him go to one of them. Ben's Place.

People expect candy store owners to be friendly and kind. Their eyes should twinkle. They should laugh like Santa Claus.

The owner of Ben's Place didn't measure up. Ben was a grizzled, crusty, foul-mouthed retired sailor who always kept a handkerchief shoved up one nostril. The hankie flapped in the breeze when Ben talked.

"Why's that handkerchief there?" a health department official had asked after Ray's mom had complained.

"I got a nose drip," Ben had replied gruffly.

"A nose drip?"

"Yep. Picked it up in some exotic place during my sailing days. My nose won't stop oozing liquid. Doubt if it ever will."

"That's disgusting!"

"Nope. Taking out this here handkerchief and letting my nose drip would be disgusting," said Ben.

The health official had been forced to agree, but he did insist that Ben change the handkerchief frequently, since he worked around food. That was all right with Ben. He had to change it frequently, anyway.

Mrs. Fanthorpe had also complained about the dust in Ben's Place, and she complained about the clouds of flies hovering over counters and landing on food. When health department official warned Ben he had to get rid of them, Ben turned the hunting of flies into a daily safari. When customers entered, Ben would be standing on the counter swinging wildly and chortling as flies dropped onto stacks of jawbreakers or piles of black licorice.

"Got one!" Ben would scream gleefully as he picked up another trophy from on top of the serviettes.

Will's mom felt sorry for Ben. She said he was a nomad, too, and he had become trapped when he bought that store. She said he was doing the only thing he could. He was trying to create a world inside one room. He was trying to find some fun in his mistake. She also said Will was never, ever, to buy anything in Ben's Place except wrapped candy and bottled soda pop.

The other candy store in the neighbourhood was Hansen's Grocery and Candy Emporium. Hansen's was immaculate in comparison. Not just in comparison with Ben's Place. In comparison with a hospital operating room or Buckingham Palace.

Every fifteen minutes Mr. Hansen, a lean man who always wore a white smock, rubber boots and hair net, would scrub up like a surgeon and put on a new pair of plastic gloves. Mr. Hansen only touched candy with tongs and tweezers, depending on size. Flies seemed to recognize that Hansen's Grocery and Candy Emporium was off limits. They never even tried to get inside.

Everything in Mr. Hansen's store was spotless except the kids who came to buy. Most of them were filthy.

Mr. Hansen made them wash up at the sinks along the back wall. If they didn't, he wouldn't sell them the licorice sticks or sets of wax teeth they craved. Kids didn't like his rules, but Hansen's was the only candy store their parents let them use.

It was only natural that Mr. Hansen should like Ray Fanthorpe. Ray was the only kid he'd ever seen who met his rigid personal standard for cleanliness and dress. Sometimes, when nobody was looking, Mr. Hansen gave Ray free candy.

"We can't cash in the bottles at Hansen's," said Will, resting one hand on the lumpy, bottle-filled backpack.

"Aw, come on. Why not?" whined Ray.

Will stood up, pulled out his bolo-bat and began to hit the ball over and over. He even bounced the ball off the thin edge of the paddle for awhile, just for a challenge.

"Mr. Hansen notices things. He'll know the bottles are old. Besides, no matter how hard we wash them, he'll find traces of dirt. He'll get suspicious."

"I'll wash them. There won't be any dirt."

"Ray?"

"Yeah?"

Will stopped paddling and stared at Ray to make the moment dramatic.

"If we take the bottles to Hansen he'll ask your mom about them. You know he will."

Ray stared back at Will.

"You're right," Ray said dejectedly, shuddering at the possibility of his mother becoming involved. "So, we have to cash them in at . . . at . . . Ben's."

"Yeah. But don't look so glum. There's one advantage to using Ben."

"What's that?"

"We don't have to wash the bottles at all," said Will with a grin. "Let's go."

No bell was mounted above the front door of Ben's Place. Ben had his own system for keeping track of customers. He never oiled hinges. His front door squeaked louder than a mouse in a cheese factory.

When Will and Ray entered the store, Ben was behind the counter, a fly swatter in one hand and both eyes glazed, following the path of his next potential victim. Ben had a silly smile on his face as he studied his prey, looking for a pattern of movement.

Will walked noisily toward the counter. Ray hesitated before sliding past rows of candy, being careful not to rub against anything. He kept glancing out the window to make sure nobody had seen him walk inside.

"What do you two want?" asked Ben, the nose hankie flapping as his eyes stayed fixed on the fly. "Don't move!" he suddenly shouted.

Will and Ray froze. Ben reached under the counter and pulled out a block of wood with a dozen nails pounded into the front edge and a dozen clothes pins mounted near the back. Rubber bands were stretched from the nails to the clothes pins.

Ben aimed the homemade rubber-band gun toward the ceiling and quickly pushed down on the back of each clothes pin in quick succession. A flurry of rubber bands twirled toward their target.

"Got him!" shouted Ben as he rushed over, picked up the tiny fly by one wing and booted him out the door like a western movie saloon-keeper kicking out a drunk.

Ray stood still, wide-eyed with terror and ready to bolt. Will picked up the rubber-band gun and inspected it. He started figuring out how many pop bottles he'd have to return to buy some clothes pins and rubber bands.

"What do you two want?" Ben asked again, leaning over to pick up rubber bands.

"We've got some pop bottles," said Will, beginning to empty his pack.

"Pop bottles! More? I'm supposed to make money, not pay it out all day long."

"More?" asked Ray.

"Yeah. Just a few minutes ago this big kid brought in about twenty bottles. Said he'd bring more tomorrow," added Ben as he counted the bottles and opened his cash drawer.

Will and Ray leaned over the counter. Some old bottles were sitting in a box pushed under a shelf. The bottles still had dirt hanging from them.

"Marty," whispered Will.

"Yeah. And Ben said he'd bring more tomorrow."

"That means he'll strike tonight. We have to stop him."

"How?"

"I don't know."

Ben counted out the refund money as his eyes began to track a new fly.

"Wouldn't it be easier to put screens on your doors and windows?" Ray couldn't help asking. "If you had screens, you wouldn't have so many flies."

"Yeah? Well, I'll tell you," said Ben with a wink as he reloaded his rubber-band shooter. "Screens might make life easier, but they wouldn't make life more fun."

Will smiled and decided his mom was right. Ben was a nomad, too.

"Can I have a couple of gum balls?" asked Will.

"Sure," said Ben, reaching into a jar with his fist and pulling out two big ones. "Here."

"Those things aren't wrapped!" warned Ray.

Will casually tossed a penny onto the counter and started swaggering toward the door. Ray was right behind him, hands still in his pockets.

"What are you doing? Those candies are filthy."

"You only live once," said Will, mimicking one of his favourite Saturday movie stars. "And I choose to lead my life dangerously. But I'll wash them first. I'm not stupid."

Will swung open the door like a movie cowboy heading for the wide-open prairie. Ray stayed hidden inside for a moment, peering out the window to make sure his parents weren't around. Next to the window was a poster. Ray read it.

"Well, hug a walnut, whatever that means," muttered Ray. "Hey, Ben? Can I have this poster?"

"Sure," said Ben, stalking his next victim. "Just don't let any flies out when you go."

Ray carefully folded the poster, making sure each corner matched perfectly. He slipped it into his back pocket and ran after his friend.

"We've got to stop Marty Robinson," snarled Will as Ray pulled up beside him. "He's going to be coming after more bottles tonight."

"I know," said Ray slowly, trying to calm Will down.

"Well, he's not getting away with it, see, Leftie," said Will, imitating his favourite movie gangster. "He'll have to drill me first." Will stopped walking for a moment and looked at Ray. "Marty could drill me, too, couldn't he?" he asked, dropping the gangster accent.

"He'll punch you right in the stomach. That's what he'll do."

"You know what this situation calls for, Ray?"

"Nope. I sure don't."

"It doesn't call for any gangster taking on some arch enemy all by himself. It calls for a western sheriff. Round up a posse for tonight, deputy," said Will, tucking his thumbs under his belt buckle and adopting a bow-legged stance.

"A posse?" asked Ray.

"So we can nab that bottle-rustling Marty Robinson."

"Sure, pard," said Ray, trying to sound like a movie sidekick. "I'll round up the gang that helped you move."

"Everyone should be at my place around dusk. Have them wait inside the garage so my parents don't see."

"We'll catch that hombre in the act," said Ray. "But remember, I don't much cotton to the idea of vigilante justice."

Will rolled his eyes. "What do you think I'm planning to do, Ray, hang Marty Robinson?"

"I don't rightly know what you have in mind there, pardner."

"I'm not real sure, either," said Will slowly, "but if there's enough of us, we'll stop him."

40

Seven

It was dark. Will, half hidden beside the porch, glanced toward the garage. Ray was there, stretching his head around the side to peer into the night. Will turned to look at the hedge near the other side of the house. Although he couldn't see them, Will knew the posse was there someplace.

Ray tossed a pebble toward Will to get his attention. Somebody was coming. Will quietly picked up his dad's flashlight and waited. A shadow opened the gate and crouched beside the walkway. Will could hear the scraping sound of someone digging.

Quietly, Will eased out from the protection of the porch. He raised the flashlight, pointed it at the shadow, and shone it straight into the face of Marty Robinson.

The flashlight had been Ray's idea. He had gotten it from some prison movie where a convict trying to escape was caught against a wall with a spotlight.

"With light in their eyes," Ray had said, "people get scared. They can't see what's behind it."

41

Will calmly stood in the safe darkness behind that beam of light and didn't say a word. He slowly started walking toward Marty Robinson, closer and closer. Marty stood up. He glanced over his shoulder. A dark figure was standing at the other side of the gate, blocking his escape. Will could hear the crunch of grass as Ray and the rest of the posse moved in tight. He knew Marty could hear it, too, and knew Marty was afraid. He could see it in his eyes.

"So," said Will, aiming the flashlight so only Marty's face was captured in its circle, "we caught you."

Marty frowned for a moment, trying to place the voice. Then his face slid into a relaxed smile.

"Oh. It's you, the McCleary kid. Is Fanthorpe with you? If he is, tell him that someday, when he's not looking, I'm going to catch him. And when I do . . ."

"We're here about your stealing, Marty," said Will coolly.

"Oh, yeah? You going to arrest me? If so, why isn't your dad here? Or even that strange mom of yours? Maybe I should call them, eh?"

"These are my bottles, Marty. The bank gave them to me."

"Oh, yeah? Then why aren't you taking them out in the daytime? And why did you cover up my holes from last night?

"Because, well, it's . . ."

"It's because your parents don't know about these bottles. Tell them about me and you've got to tell them about the bottles, too. Right?"

Marty wasn't slow when it came to doing things wrong.

Will didn't say a thing. He couldn't. When he'd planned the ambush it had seemed so easy. He knew the feeling of being caught. When it happened to him he meekly admitted guilt and was sorry. Marty was different. Marty had been caught. He was wrong. He was outnumbered. But he was cowering everyone else. It wasn't supposed to work that way.

"Tell you what, jerk," said Marty.

"Yeah?"

"I'm going to give you a chance."

"What do you mean?"

"You got four choices. Here they are."

Marty Robinson took a quick step to one side. He struck a finger into the flashlight beam.

"One. I shout for your parents, and we explain things to them. They might get mad at me. I don't care. I don't have to live with them. They will definitely get mad at you." He shook his finger at Will. "You've been keeping secrets. Parents hate secrets more than anything else. Anything.

"Two," continued Marty, unfolding another finger. "Nothing changes. I keep taking bottles whenever I want. You keep getting up early to cover up so your parents don't get wise.

"Three," he said, adding another finger. "Give me twenty-five bottles a week and I won't take any others, promise. I make you this deal so I don't have to dig in dirt at night.

"Four."

Slowly, a fourth finger appeared in the circle of light. Marty held it there for a moment without saying a word.

"We fight. Beat me and I leave you alone. The bottles are yours, promise. I beat you, and all the pop bottles are mine. You can't take any, and you have to cover the holes." Marty's fingers sank out of the light. "What'll it be?"

Will began to shiver. The flashlight shook in his hand. He was the good guy. He was supposed to win.

"We'll fight," said Ray calmly from behind Will.

Will turned to stare at his friend. "What . . ."

"We'll fight?" broke in Marty. "What's this We? I haven't forgotten about you, Fanthorpe. I'm going to fight you, too, but not tonight. This fight is between McCleary and me."

"He'll fight, then," said Ray.

"No, I won't!"

"Yes, you will. And according to the international rules of duelling, the challenged party has the right to choose both the type of weapon and the means of combat.''

''Weapons?'' exclaimed Will, his voice rising in terror.

''Go ahead, choose,'' said Marty, flexing his muscles.

Ray reached into his back pocket and pulled out the poster he'd picked up at Ben's Place. Will shone the flashlight onto it so they could all read.

BOLO BAT CONTEST

The Vancouver Parks Board, in co-operation with the Loyola Theatre, announces a citywide Bolo-Bat competition. Area contests will be held at community parks on Saturday, August 5th. Area winners will perform between features at the Saturday Loyola matinee, August 12th. The person who can bat the longest wins a brand-new bicycle.

Contact your local community centre, public library, or the Loyola box office for local contest times and details.

Will stared at the poster. A bike. He'd never even ridden a bicycle. He didn't know anyone who had ridden a bicycle. To actually think about owning a bike had always seemed as crazy as wishing to be a hero in the Old West. Some things just didn't happen. But now. There was nobody better with a bolo-bat. Will was sure of that. There couldn't be.

"Bolo-bats?" asked Marty Robinson. "We're supposed to hit each other with bolo-bats?"

"Not each other," said Ray, holding up his own finger. "The ball. That's all you get to hit, the little red ball. The challenged party in a duel gets to choose weapons and the means of combat.

"Each of you is to enter this contest, but at different parks. If either one of you doesn't make it to the finals, that person loses. If you both make it to the finals, the one who bats the longest up there on the Loyola stage wins the bottles. That's the duel."

Will waited for Marty to rip up the poster and demand a real fight. He prayed Marty would be suckered into competing with the best bolo-bat paddler alive.

Will shone the flashlight at Marty's face. Marty was grinning. Suddenly, a wooden bolo-bat rose into the spotlight. Will moved back a couple of steps so the beam showed all of Marty Robinson. Marty was holding a bolo-bat. He swung his paddle and hit the little red ball. The ball sailed into the dark and then came speeding back. Marty hit it again and again, establishing a rhythm. Marty hit the ball twice with the side of his paddle, once with his elbow, twice off his knee, and then swivelled around and batted the ball behind his back without looking.

"Sure," said Marty. "It's a duel."

Marty Robinson casually walked out of the spotlight, trading his bolo-bat from hand to hand between hits. The sound of rubber hitting wood disappeared into the night.

"Well," mumbled Ray. "At least you've got a chance. You wouldn't have had a chance in any other kind of fight."

"Yeah," agreed Will absently, trying to figure out how anyone could paddle without looking. "Ray?" he asked.

"Yeah?"

"How come we've never seen Marty with a bolo-bat?"

Ray shrugged. "I guess because we're never behind him. We're always in front, running. I've never even seen his back pocket."

"Ray?"

"Yeah?"

"The good guys always win. Right?"

"Sure. At least . . . they do in movies."

THE CONTEST

Eight

When Will and Ray arrived at Mt. Pleasant Park, there was a huge circle of contestants and spectators. Will registered and unravelled his elastic string. The contest judge was a big teenager with a large stomach. He blew on his whistle and called all the competitors to a small rise in front of an outstretched rope. Ray patted Will on the back. Will nodded and walked slowly toward the group of batters.

The judge read the rules. There weren't many. The ball had to hit the paddle every time it bounced back. That was the main one.

Will raised his hand.

"Yes?" asked the judge.

"Can we use the side of the paddle?" asked Will.

"No!" shouted Ray. "Play it safe! Please!"

"The ball just has to hit the wood of the paddle," said the judge. "Miss and you're out. No arguments. The winner will represent Mt. Pleasant Park at the

Loyola next week. The winner of that contest will get the new bike. All right, get ready.''

The sixty competitors spread out, forming a long, weaving line stretching halfway across the park. They gave each other lots of room so elastics wouldn't accidentally tangle.

The judge blew his whistle. Everyone began to bat. The crowd was quiet. All anyone could hear was the off-beat drumming of little rubber balls hitting wood, over and over. Most of the contestants weren't good. They'd entered with hopes of a miracle and dreams of a bicycle, but little skill.

Within ten minutes only two competitors were left, Will and a girl named Lori. Lori used a tongue out, total concentration style. Will knew her name because somebody in the audience kept chanting it in time with her hits. Lori was about thirty feet away and a little in front of Will. He saw her when she began to struggle. From the crowd Will and Lori looked like two spinning tops, one steady and the other beginning to wobble. To make things interesting, Will hit his ball with a paddle edge.

"Stop!" yelled Ray.

He said it with such command that Will did stop hitting the ball with the edge of his paddle. Lori heard him, too, and she stopped paddling completely. Lori looked up, puzzled, trying to find out why she'd been ordered to quit.

"The winner!" shouted the judge, rushing over to lift Will's arm like he'd just won a knock-out decision in some boxing match. Will closed his eyes, listening to the cheers and pretending he'd just flattened Marty Robinson.

"Who yelled stop?" asked Lori loudly, shielding her eyes with her paddle. Her elastic string swung back and forth in front of her nose as she searched through the crowd. Ray meekly raised his hand.

"I did," he admitted. Fanthorpes never lied.

"Aren't you his friend?" Lori asked, pointing at Will. She stood so close to Ray that she was stepping on the toes of his well-polished shoes.

"Yeah. But I only yelled because Will was using the side of his paddle. I . . . I didn't mean . . ."

"I could have won!" Lori yelled.

Ray tried to move away from her but couldn't without scraping the tops of his shoes.

"Hold on," interrupted the judge. "No fighting. This kid's the winner," he added, pushing Will toward Lori.

Will gulped. Lori was holding her paddle as if she were capable of hitting more than a tiny red ball. He nodded. She scowled.

"Wait! I want to be fair," said Will, staring into Lori's eyes. "We'll do it again. Just the two of us. Beat me and you can have my spot in the finals."

"Deal!" said Lori.

"No," shouted Ray. "Are you crazy, Will? We've got more at stake here than a dumb contest or bicycle."

"You don't have to do this," said the judge.

"I know."

"The rules state a competitor loses when stopping for any reason. She stopped."

"I can beat her," said Will.

Lori smiled.

"Prove it," she said.

Ray moaned and sat down on the grass. Will and Lori began to paddle. Lori was determined not to lose again. Her tongue was set, her eyes focused. Together, side by side, Will and Lori paddled for twenty minutes, then thirty and forty-five.

Will wasn't trying any fancy tricks now. He used a calm, steady stroke, a circular wrist motion, hit and swing. Will started to sweat. He could feel wetness building up on the handle of his paddle.

The two kept paddling, each hoping the other would make a mistake. Will's arm began to tire. It was usually an easy move to switch the paddle to his right hand, but Will was nervous. He started the switch. Too slow. As he planted the paddle in his right palm the ball bounced back and hit the edge. The ball veered off at an odd angle. Will had to reach for a couple of shots before regaining his rhythm.

Lori saw the switch from the corner of her eye. She switched hands, too, smoothly.

"One hour!" called out the judge in awe.

The contest ended two minutes later. Lori missed. She missed on purpose. She calmly stopped paddling, nabbed her ball, quickly spun the elastic cord around her paddle handle, and ran out of the park. It happened so fast that Will didn't even notice. He kept on paddling. The audience didn't say anything for a moment. Everyone was stunned. They'd settled in for a marathon match and expected, at the very least, a scream of disappointment. After a few moments the judge blew his whistle, and the crowd cheered for Will.

Will sort of half collapsed and turned to shake hands with Lori. She wasn't there.

"The winner!" yelled the judge again, shoving a special free movie ticket into Will's empty hand.

"Where's Lori?" Will asked. "I'd like to meet her."

"Oh, she had to leave, I guess," said the judge.

"Was she upset at having lost?"

"Uh, I guess so. Sure, that must have been it."

Ray ducked under the rope and came racing toward Will, all smiles and relief.

"Hug a walnut," said Will. "I did it."

"Yeah, but don't scare me like that again."

"What happened to Lori?"

"I don't know. She just left. Don't worry about her, though. You're in training, buddy. We've got work to do. Next week you bat for everything. And you bat against Marty Robinson."

Nine

Ray sat on the back steps of Will's house with a cardboard megaphone pressed against his lips.

"Stroke! Stroke!" he yelled.

Between shouts Ray chewed gum. The smacking sound echoed through the megaphone.

Will stood on the pop-bottle walkway, hitting his little red ball to the beat of Ray's voice.

"I brought some lemonade," said Will's mom, kicking open the back door with her foot. She paused and smiled. "I'm off to see the mountains. This just may be my last trip by bus, though." She set the lemonade next to Ray. "I have a plan for getting a car. Bye."

Will and Ray didn't pay much attention. Anna McCleary always had plans for getting a car.

"Stroke! Stroke! Stroke!" shouted Ray, reaching for a glass filled with ice-cold lemonade. He drank some, and the slurping sound was magnified by the homemade bullhorn.

"Would you stop torturing me with food sounds?" blurted Will.

"You've got to practise. Marty won his contest. He batted for more than two hours. And that Lori girl almost beat you."

"She didn't, though. She ran away." Will didn't add that he was sorry Lori had left. He wanted to meet her. She sure could paddle and she sure could stand up for herself and she sure was something else, too, but he wasn't sure what. It made Will feel funny to think about it.

"Concentrate!"

Will almost missed a shot. He dived to the grass and hit the ball a couple of inches above the ground. He rolled over quickly to make the next hit, sprang up, and recovered.

"Okay. Break!" yelled Ray into his megaphone, like a movie director stopping a scene.

Will quit paddling and dropped to the grass, flat on his back with his arms spread wide. One hand fell onto the smooth glass of a bottle bottom. He circled it caressingly with his fingers.

"Geez, you almost missed," said Ray, standing over Will.

"Not really."

"What do you mean? I saw you. That was close."

"I did it on purpose."

"What?"

Will turned onto his stomach.

"I just read this interview with Charlie Chaplin. Chaplin says perfection isn't exciting. Good jugglers get more applause when they almost miss. People like them more. So, they practise making mistakes. I've been practising, too. He's right. You were bored. Then, I almost missed."

"Don't ever do it again," said Ray. "But now that you mention it, I've been thinking. That movie theatre can't let a bunch of kids paddle away for two hours between films. You know matinee audiences. They'll rip the place apart."

"I could throw in some almost missing to keep it exciting."

"No!"

"Just kidding. You worry too much, Ray. Who cares what the audience thinks? Those theatre people just didn't know there were paddlers as good as me, or Marty. Too bad. I'm going to beat Marty. I'll paddle perfectly for three hours if that's what it takes."

"I suppose you're right. Tell you what. Ten more push-ups and we'll take the rest of the day off."

"We'll take it off? I'm the one doing all the work," muttered Will as he rolled onto the pop-bottle walkway and put each palm on top of a glass bottom, ready for the push-ups.

"ONE," Ray shouted through the megaphone as Will fought his way up. "TWO . . . and remember . . . THREE . . . you're coming to my house for dinner . . . FOUR . . . I mean, your parents' cooking is probably great . . . FIVE . . . but the book on athletic training I got from the . . . SIX . . . library says that on the night before some . . . SEVEN . . . big event, you should eat spaghetti, and my dad . . . EIGHT . . . makes great spaghetti so . . . NINE . . . be there at six . . . TEN.''

"6:10?" asked Will, collapsing onto the pop bottles.

"No, six. The ten was for the last push-up."

"I know," said Will grinning. "It was a joke."

Ray rolled his eyes.

"Don't be late. My mom has a . . . surprise for you."

"Your mom? I didn't think she liked me."

Ray thought for a moment.

"She doesn't," he admitted, staring at Will. "And I'm glad you know that. It'll help."

"What do you mean?"

"You won't think this surprise is terrific," said Ray quietly, staring at his feet and shuffling dirt with his polished shoes. "Tonight, you're going to find out more about me and my family than I ever would have told you. Just remember that none of this was my idea. All right?"

"Sure," replied Will, because he couldn't think of anything else to say. He slapped Ray on the shoulder like buddies are supposed to do and smiled.

Will tried to look his best for the Fanthorpe dinner. He wore pants with no patches on the knees. They were his school pants. The patch was in the back, on the bum. It got there from the twisting Will did on hard wooden seats. Will figured one patch on the bum was better than two on the knees. He could probably keep Ray's parents from standing behind him and noticing.

Will put on his father's belt. It was too long for him, though, and the cloth loops on his trousers were too narrow to send it around twice. The loose end waved out to one side.

He also wore his one white shirt and his leather shoes. The shoes were a size too small and made him walk funny. His parents were waiting until the fall to buy a new pair. They were hoping Will's feet would do their growing in the summer, like a crop, and then hibernate all winter long. From the pain in his feet Will knew at least part of the plan was working. His feet had definitely grown.

Will's mom insisted he take something to the Fanthorpes, since they were feeding him dinner.

"It's only fair," she said, handing him a bowl filled with greyish pudding.

Will liked grey pudding. His mom had learned to make it in the desert. He'd never asked what its odd-sounding name meant in English. He was afraid of finding out. It was a delicacy Will chose to relish in ignorance.

Will knew grey pudding was not a gift the Fanthorpes were likely to enjoy, or even try. So, after leaving by the front door, he sneaked around to the garage, hid the pudding bowl, nabbed a trowel and quickly dug up five pop bottles from the back walkway. He planted a couple of broken bottles in their place and ran to Hansen's Candy and Grocery Emporium. Will washed the bottles and himself at a sink along Hansen's back wall, and then cashed in the bottles for four Sweet Marie candy bars.

He didn't know what else to take as a present. Candy seemed an appropriate gift for any occasion, and Will wanted to make a good impression. He didn't even run from the store to Ray's house, partly because he didn't want to sweat and partly because his shoes were too tight. This was the first time Will had ever been invited into the Fanthorpe house.

"Good evening, Master McCleary," said Ray's mom, opening the front door and inspecting Will. Will tried to peek over her shoulder to see inside.

"Mrs. Fanthorpe," Will said proudly, holding out the four candy bars, "my mom sent these for dessert. They're a gift."

"Candy . . . bars!" sputtered Mrs. Fanthorpe with surprise. "Why, thank you," she added coolly, gently closing the door behind Will.

"Hi," said Ray.

Will turned, and his smile froze. On every wall, almost like wallpaper, were huge floor-to-ceiling oil portraits surrounded by heavy gold-coloured frames. The men and women in the paintings wore austere expressions. Will felt kind of creepy. He had seen a horror movie once in which the bad guys spied on the good guys through tiny holes in the eyes of portraits just like these.

"You get used to it," said Ray calmly. "They're partly why I've never invited you inside before."

"Who are they?" Will managed to croak.

"They're my ancestors," said Ray formally.

Will tried to stop staring at the paintings. Ray and his dad stood beside a couch in the middle of the room. Both were dressed for dinner. They wore sweaters, ties and freshly pressed pants.

"Before the Depression," said Ray, "we lived in a big house with lots of furniture and three full-time servants. I can't remember much about it. We lost our money when the stock market crashed. We got to keep these portraits, though. Nobody wanted them."

"We'll have our money back some day," added Mrs. Fanthorpe. "There are lawsuits. In the meantime we are attempting to raise Raymond as a true Fanthorpe. Then, when we regain our fortune, Raymond can step into his rightful position of authority."

"Well," said Mr. Fanthorpe, changing the subject, "I suppose you lads are excited about tomorrow. We plan to attend, although I understand movie theatres don't take reservations. People are supposed to wait in line. Odd. Still, we'll be there. Raymond has taken great pride in preparing you, William, for this contest of . . . skill. We have encouraged him, frankly. After all, the Fanthorpes have always been great horse trainers. In our stable we had . . . "

"Which brings us to the point of this little gathering," interrupted Ray's mom. "First, though, William must promise never to tell a soul what he is to learn."

Will looked quizzically at Ray. Ray nodded.

"I swear," said Will softly.

"Ray? Sweetheart?" said Mrs. Fanthorpe dramatically. "Lift up your sweaters!"

Ray and his father looked at each other and timed their lifts so neither had to expose what was underneath his sweater first. Will couldn't believe what he saw. Each shirt was a crazy quilt of stray material sewn together like some ridiculous jigsaw puzzle. The shirts looked like they had been pieced together by a mad seamstress run amuck. Will stared, his mouth open.

"Hug a walnut," he said slowly.

"Take off your sweaters now," ordered Mrs. Fanthorpe.

Ray and his father pulled their sweaters over their heads in perfect unison and turned to model their shirts. The only parts of each shirt that matched were the collars, the cuffs and the sleeves.

"Get the others," said Mrs. Fanthorpe.

Ray folded his sweater and draped it carefully over the back of the couch. He left the room and came back a moment later carrying an armload of perfectly ironed shirts. Each one was a bizarre creation of scraps. All had perfectly matched sleeves and collars.

"We are a poor family now . . . " said Mr. Fanthorpe.

"Temporarily," added his wife.

" . . . but Ray's mother and I were raised to respect the value of being well-dressed. Unfortunately, we cannot afford quality clothes at the moment."

"But," broke in Mrs. Fanthorpe, "we can still create the illusion of being well dressed. Raymond owns two good sweaters and a great many shirts made from garment factory scraps. The factory gives the material to me, and they give me collars and cuffs with minor imperfections. They do it because we used to own the factory. I sew all the pieces together."

"That's why Ray always wears sweaters!" muttered Will. "He has to hide the shirts."

"That's it," admitted Ray.

"Why tell me?"

"Because," said Mrs. Fanthorpe, "and I mean no offence, but you dress like a hobo, a tramp. You are a most repugnant sight."

"So?" said Will, turning red. "I dress the same as every other kid around here, except Ray."

"Exactly!" exclaimed Mr. Fanthorpe. "Now you've hit the problem. And, as you have become one of our son's projects, and as we intend to watch you represent the entire Mt. Pleasant section of town at that theatre tomorrow . . ."

"Yeah?"

"We would like to loan you a sweater, a shirt and a bow tie."

"And some shoes, too," added Mrs. Fanthorpe, pointing at Will's feet and wrinkling her nose.

"Please take them," pleaded Ray.

Will gulped. He wanted to scream "No!" and run out the front door. Will looked up at all the ancestral eyes staring at him. He looked at Ray's eyes, alive and pleading. Ray was his friend, and Ray was stuck. Heroes always helped their friends.

"Okay, Why not?" said Will slowly. "But no bow tie. I have to be comfortable if I'm going to win."

"We wouldn't want to compromise your chance

at victory," said Mr. Fanthorpe as he clapped his hands together and began to rub them.

"Shall we eat?" asked Mrs. Fanthorpe sweetly, speeding along Will's visit.

CONTEST MORNING

Ten

Will finished buttoning the patchwork shirt Ray had loaned him and then slipped the navy-blue sweater over his head. He was taller than Ray, so there wasn't much extra length. Will tugged at the bottom of the sweater to make sure his shirt wouldn't show, took a deep breath and sauntered into the kitchen.

"Wow!" said Will's dad, half laughing. "That sure is some outfit. Those the clothes Ray's parents gave you to wear?"

"Yeah. Like them?"

"You going to be comfortable?"

"I think so," said Will, standing at the counter and putting together a sandwich. "You and Mom coming to watch?"

"Of course."

"But we can't walk down there with you," said his mom.

"Why not?"

"Oh, we have some . . . uh . . . things to take care of."

"What kind of things?" asked Will, not really interested.

"Never you mind," said his mom. If Will had looked up, he would have seen her eyes sparkle. "You'll find out. In the meantime, take your paddle and get going."

Will crammed the last of the sandwich into his mouth, nabbed his bolo-bat from the top of a cupboard, and shoved it into his back pocket.

"We'll be there cheering for you," yelled Mr. McCleary as Will rushed out the back door.

Will sat on the bottom step and pulled on his sneakers. He reached down and touched the walkway, cleaning the dust off a bottle and tracing along its rim for good luck. He was going off to fight for his bottles, and he was going to win.

"You ready?" asked Ray, standing by the side of the house. Ray was wearing a blue sweater, too, but he and Will didn't look like twins. Ray wore his clothes with respect. Will treated clothes like they were only a convenient place to keep change and wipe his hands.

"Ready," said Will, casting one last, long look at all the glass bottle bottoms.

"Let's go, then."

66

They walked across the Cambie Street Bridge and into downtown Vancouver. They walked confidently. They were on their way to the Saturday afternoon movie matinee, where the good guys always won.

The line-up in front of the Loyola stretched around the block. Will and Ray walked to the end of the line, greeting friends and accepting pats on the back for good luck. Ray fished in his pockets to dig out the six cents admission. Will gripped his special ticket.

Inside, Will and Ray tramped down an aisle. Up on stage, under a spotlight, was a brand-new, bright-red bicycle with white-walled tires and plastic multi-coloured streamers hanging from the handlebar grips. It was beautiful.

"Don't look," said Ray, taking Will by the arm. "You'll get too nervous."

Other than the spot-lit bike, it was a typical matinee. The theatre was filled with screaming kids throwing popcorn and chocolate bars. A few hundred were trying to spin flattened popcorn containers into the chandeliers so they'd stick. Will and Ray sat near the front, a couple of rows behind Marty Robinson. Marty was by himself. He got mad at anybody who tried to sit too close.

"Are you sure your parents want to come here?" Will asked as a candy-bar wrapper whistled past his ear.

"Geez," muttered Ray, "I never thought about them actually sitting through a movie. I just pictured them watching the contest."

"Too late," said Will, slouching down in his seat. "They're here." He nodded toward the back of the theatre.

Mr. and Mrs. Fanthorpe stood silhouetted at the entrance. They were dressed for the opening night of a Broadway play. Mr. Fanthorpe wore a tuxedo, top hat, scarf and gloves. He carried a cane, even though Will had never seen him limp. Mrs. Fanthorpe wore a sequined gown, high heels and a wide-brimmed hat.

Ray's parents strolled regally down the aisle, searching for some corner of sanity. The screaming battle raging around them seemed to recognize they were innocents in the fray. Where they walked no popcorn flew. Shouts turned to silence as the entire audience stopped their matinee warm-up to stare.

"They're going to get massacred," muttered Ray. "How long can this mob of sharpshooters resist a target like Dad's top hat?"

Mr. Fanthorpe found two aisle seats and gently brushed them off with his handkerchief before escorting his wife to her place.

"Hey," whispered a girl behind Will, "I think that's Fred Astaire and Ginger Rogers, the movie stars."

Most of the kids in the balcony were perched over the rails, staring down. Miraculously, none of them seemed tempted to drop candy bars on Mr. Fanthorpe's top hat. He looked too much like a hero from the movies.

Will and Ray looked at each other and giggled.

"They're going to be all right," said Ray with relief.

"I guess if people do things differently, they should do them with style."

"Shh. The movie's starting. You're on after the first feature."

The lights dimmed. The audience cheered. Will and Ray settled back to crunch popcorn and watch. It was a western. The good guys winning was never a concern. All worry centred around the fate of an old prospector. Will didn't really care that much. He was only partly watching. He kept smoothing his sweater and thinking about where he would ride that bike.

Will figured the first thing he'd do, right away, would be to wheel the bike out to the street in front of the theatre. He'd let his friends try to ride. Then he'd ride it himself. He was sure he could. Riding a bike didn't look hard. He'd ride it home, slowly, so he could stay with Ray. He'd keep it in his room and on Sundays he'd ride that bike down Burrard Street to the ocean, his hair flying back from the wind.

He'd feel speed, see new places, explore. He'd use that bike just like his mom said she wanted to use a car. "You know," Will muttered in himself, "maybe there's a bit of nomad in me, too."

It made him feel proud to think so.

"Shh," whispered Ray. "It's almost time."

On the screen the last cow was being herded into a corral beside the railroad tracks. The hero was sitting on his horse while the rancher rode up to congratulate him. Will was relieved to see the old prospector perched on a mule. He had lived.

As the hero and rancher's daughter rode off together, the theatre manager, wearing a red jacket and blue pants with a black satin stripe down each leg, marched on stage.

"Well," he shouted into a microphone as the curtain closed and the lights came on, "it's now time for the finals of our city-wide bolo-bat championship. The twenty area champs should bring their bats and come on up here!"

"You can do it," said Ray quietly. "Don't let anything stop you."

Will stood up and turned toward the aisle. There in front of him stood Lori, the girl he'd only just managed to beat the week before.

"Hi," she said, smiling. "Quite an outfit you're

wearing. Hope you've been practising. I have. And this time I'm going to beat you."

"Hug a walnut!" said Will.

Eleven

"You!"

"Me," admitted Lori with a smile, holding up her paddle for Will to see.

"But I beat you."

"No. I quit."

"Same thing."

"No. I left on purpose. I am the Britannia Park champ."

"I don't understand."

"It's simple. The Britannia contest started later. I figured there was a better chance of winning there, so I quit."

"You hear that, Will?" broke in Ray. "She didn't think she could beat you. Don't let this bother you."

"It won't. I have been practising," he told Lori.

"Good luck, then."

"Good luck to you."

"Are all the competitors here?" asked the theatre manager.

"Hold on! Two more!" shouted Ray, pointing at Will and Lori as they raced down the aisle together and tramped up the three short steps to the stage.

Will tried to look out at the crowd to find his parents. A spotlight partly blinded him. Will glanced down at where he'd have to stare when he was paddling. Another spotlight glared back. Will squinted and looked along the ragged line-up of park champions. All of them, even Marty Robinson, were squinting. The lights had been positioned to keep batters blinded so the match would be short.

"Okay. Here are the rules," yelled out the theatre manager, but Will wasn't paying attention. The lights were more than bright. They were hot, and Will was wearing a wool sweater. He couldn't concentrate on bolo-batting if he was dripping sweat. Will's hand reached for the bottom of his sweater, but then he stopped. Under that sweater was not a normal shirt. Everyone would laugh if they saw it, and Ray's parents would be furious.

"People won't laugh if I win," muttered Will to himself. "Ray said not to let anything stop me."

Will dropped his paddle to the stage, reached down and nabbed the bottom of the sweater with both hands.

"No!" cried out Mrs. Fanthorpe.

Will hesitated for a moment and then pulled the sweater over his head. He dropped the sweater and stood on stage wearing Ray's crazy, patched shirt.

The audience grew quiet for the second time that afternoon, a record never again to be matched at a Vancouver Saturday afternoon movie matinee. In that moment of silence Will heard Mrs. Fanthorpe sigh, and he heard his mother laugh. She was laughing like Will had planned to do something funny.

The whole audience began to laugh, too. Will smiled and did a slow, tiptoe spin, like a model showing off some fancy suit.

"If everyone is quite ready," said the theatre manager irritably, staring at Will. "Begin when you hear the music."

The manager nodded to someone off stage. From the giant theatre speakers came a series of hisses and pops as a phonograph needle touched a record.

Will groaned. The volume was turned up all the way to bother the batters. The speakers were right behind the screen.

Will gripped his paddle tightly. The theatre manager blew his whistle, and the first note of a brass band march, played at double time, blared out of the speakers. The entire audience crunched hands over ears. Some of the paddlers on stage did the same thing, instinctively protecting themselves as they raced off stage.

Will started paddling. So did Lori and Marty Robinson and three or four others.

From the back of the theatre a group of kids yelled out, "Marty Robinson's going to lose!"

Marty got mad and started to look up to see who was shouting so he could get them later, but he stopped himself. He was in a contest.

"Marty Robinson's going to lose!" the group yelled again and again, making it into a chant.

"Marty Robinson's going to lose!" chanted everyone in the theatre Marty had ever bullied, which meant everyone except Will and Ray's parents, the ushers, the popcorn vendor and the theatre manager.

"Marty Robinson's going to lose! Marty Robinson's going to lose!" everyone kept shouting, so loud that even the march music seemed soft. Marty looked up, hoping to quiet the audience by picking out one or two kids for dark, menacing stares. The lights blinded him, and he tried to shield his eyes with his paddling hand. The little red ball whizzed past, missing wood.

The theatre manager jogged quickly over to Marty and yelled, "You're out!" like a baseball umpire. Marty didn't budge. He stared at nothing, his mouth open. The manager took Marty by an arm and began to lead him from the stage. Marty's paddle hung by his side, the little red ball bouncing behind him.

"Loser! Loser!" chanted the audience.

Will grinned and began to relax. He had won the bottles. Now for the bike.

"Loser! Loser!" he chanted in time with each smack of his little red ball.

"Loser! Loser!" the theatre mob kept chanting as Marty Robinson disappeared behind curtains at the side of the stage.

"Loser! Loser!" said Will softly as he slid into stride. He was the best, and he knew it. Bright lights and loud music weren't going to bother Will McCleary.

Within a few minutes there were only three competitors left. Then two. Will and Lori. Together, in perfect rhythm, they hit and hit. Over and over.

It wasn't long before Lori began to reach for shots, and Will knew he had the bicycle won. Confidently, he switched hands twice. He hit the ball behind his back, without looking. The audience cheered. Lori kept struggling, getting wilder with each hit.

Will deftly brought his paddle back in front and began to hit the ball with the edge. A bike! He was going to win a brand-new bike! He couldn't possibly lose. To make sure, Will settled back into a regular pace, waiting patiently for Lori to miss.

Then, as Will's wrist twisted perfectly into place for another shot, prepared to feel that ball slap against his paddle, he felt nothing at all.

No ball. It hadn't come back. His long, thin, faithful elastic used for so many hours of patient practice chose just that moment to snap in two. One weightless piece of elastic dangled from Will's paddle. The other trailed behind his little red ball as it arced up and away like a beautifully hit home run.

Will's eyes widened in horror as he watched his ball travel higher and higher, almost in slow motion, and then vanish into the darkness of the theatre.

Twelve

"The winner!" shouted the theatre manager as he wheeled the shiny red bike past Will toward Lori. Will kept staring at the spot where his little red ball had disappeared. In his mind it was still climbing, a miniature rubber and elastic comet.

Whoosh. He'd lost.

Lori gripped her bike by the handlebars and waved to the cheering crowd. Will breathed deeply for a moment, choking back tears. Slowly, he bent down and picked up Ray's sweater. He paused and then gently placed his broken paddle on the stage floor. Will left it there and slunk quietly off the stage. Nobody tried to stop him or say anything as he walked up the dark aisle toward the back of the theatre.

"You can stay for the next movie if you'd like," said the usher at the entrance. "It's free."

Will held back tears, shook his head and walked out into the bright afternoon light. He squinted and breathed deeply again.

"I lost," he admitted to himself. "But I'm a good guy. Elastics don't break for the good guys. Good guys always . . ."

"Congratulations!" said Ray, slapping Will on the back.

"Congratulations?"

"The pop bottles. They're all yours. You beat Marty Robinson. He won't dare bother us now."

"Do you have to be so . . . so cheery, Ray?"

"Just trying to help. You know, silver lining and all that stuff."

"But I should have won, Ray. It isn't fair." Will stopped for a moment to catch his breath. "Sorry about taking off the sweater," he added. "The lights were hot, you see, and . . ."

"Don't worry about it. Besides, my parents love this place. Kids are lined up asking for their autographs . . ."

"Hurrah!" shouted a mob of kids behind Ray and Will. Pushing through them was a brand-new bicycle. Lori was grinning and laughing and offering rides to everyone. She saw Will and rolled the bike over to him. The mob stayed back.

"Too bad about your ball," said Lori, and she seemed serious, too.

"I would have won, you know," said Will.

"Maybe."

"You were struggling."

"Not really. I was just making the contest more interesting. See, I read this interview with Charlie Chaplin and . . ."

"You were almost missing on purpose?"

"Sure."

"No, you weren't."

"Oh, yeah? Tell you what. You gave me another chance, so I'll give you one. Meet me tomorrow. Mt. Pleasant Park at noon."

"Do I get the bike if I win?"

Lori smiled and held the bike a little tighter. "No. But even if you lose you can ride it all you want. Every day. And if you do beat me I'll tell everyone you're the real champ."

Will blushed.

"Okay," he said, trying to smile. "It's a deal. And I'm going to win, too."

"How can you be so sure?"

"Didn't you know?" said Will, pointing to himself. "Good guys always win."

"Will?"

"Yeah?"

"Hate to tell you this, but I'm a good guy, too. Bring a new paddle, eh? You're going to need one."

Lori turned back toward the crowd, showing off the bike.

"Don't worry about the bike," said Ray. "Buy your own with pop-bottle money."

"Will! Will!" shouted his parents as they fought their way through the bicycle mob.

"Sorry you lost, son," said his dad.

"That's all right, really."

Will looked at his mom. She didn't look sad. She was beaming.

"Mom, what is it?" asked Will.

"I'm sorry you lost, Will. But I've got a surprise that might make the day a little better for you."

"What is it?"

"Come on over here and see," said Anna Mc-Cleary mysteriously.

Will looked up at his dad. He nodded. Will and Ray followed Anna McCleary part way down the block. She stopped suddenly.

"What do you see?" she asked.

Will looked around. He didn't see much. It was a normal, busy, downtown street. He looked at his mom and shrugged. She held up her key ring and pointed to the keys one at a time. There was a house key, a key to the church where she taught piano lessons and . . . and another key. Anna McCleary leaned against a ten-year-old Model T Ford and ran her free hand along one bumper.

"A car? You bought a car?" asked Will.

His mom nodded. "It's the Westerby car."

Will and Ray leaped onto the running board to peek inside. They were both excited.

"How could you afford it?"

"It was like a gift, sort of. Besides, we got it cheap. It needs work and the Westerbys need money," said Anna McCleary.

She unlocked the doors. Will and Ray hopped into the back seat, laughing and cheering. Will's parents slid into the front, his mom at the wheel.

"Let's drive home so you can change shirts, Will," suggested his mom. "I thought I'd die laughing when you took off that sweater. Ray?"

"Yes, Mrs. McCleary?"

"Do you always wear shirts like that?"

"Yes, Mrs. McCleary," said Ray sheepishly.

"Then you have a smart mom. Tell her I said so."

"I will!"

"After Will changes, we'll all drive up to Cypress Park for a view of the city."

Will kicked off his shoes. They hurt. He pulled Ray's shirt over his head so he wouldn't waste time at home. The only time Will had ever ridden in a car was during a move once. And he had never seen the mountains up close. It was turning into a good day, sort of. He'd met Lori again, won the pop bottles and was going to the mountains in a car. Anna McCleary coaxed the well-worn Ford into gear and carefully eased into the street.

The old Ford pulled up in front of the McCleary house. Will hopped out and started running. He was halfway between the sidewalk and the porch before he realized his bare feet were not striding over cool, smooth rings of glass.

He was running over dirt and mud.

Will braked to a stop and looked down. The lawn looked like it had been attacked by a herd of gophers. There were holes and dirt everywhere. The pop bottles were gone.

Will turned to his parents. Ray was behind them, staring at the ground with his mouth open wide.

"The walkway?" Will managed to stutter.

"Isn't it great?" yelled Jim McCleary.

"Great?" asked Will, swallowing hard.

"Yeah," said his mom. "You know me, always looking around, up and down, all over. It's a shame more people don't notice what's right in front of them, at their feet, even."

Will couldn't look at his parents. He stared down at the ground.

"Anyway," broke in Will's dad, "just guess what the walkway in front of this house . . ."

"And the back patio," added his mom.

" . . . and the back patio were made of. Guess."

Will's toes reached out to search for missed pop bottles. All they touched was dirt.

"Bottles!" said his dad.

"So?"

"So they're worth money!" said Will's mom. "I figured it all out the day we moved here. And you know how?"

"How?"

"It was those kids who helped us move. They took off their shoes, remember?"

"Yeah."

"I figured, what the heck, and so I took off my shoes, too. The walkway felt kind of funny so I bent down, took a close look, and noticed all those bottles. I went to the bank a couple of days later and tried to see the manager. A funny fellow. He wouldn't even listen to me. I said, 'pop bottles,' and he smiled and kept saying, 'Keep 'em. Keep 'em.' So we did."

"Ben bought them from us," said Will's dad. "You should have seen his face when we told him we had 4,356 bottles to cash in. I had to tell him a couple of days ago, of course, so he'd be ready with the money. We dug up the bottles this morning after you left. Cashed them in and bought the car. We wanted it to be a surprise for you."

"You are surprised, aren't you?" asked Anna McCleary.

"Yeah, I'm surprised," muttered Will. "I'm really, really, really surprised."

Ray still stood by the gate, staring down at the torn-up walkway. Will turned and walked up the porch steps and into the house.

"I couldn't be any more surprised," Will said out loud as he walked into his room. He tried not to cry as he slipped on one of his own shirts. He looked into the mirror.

"I, William McCleary, must have the only mother in the whole world who still looks at the world like a kid. Terrific."

The car horn beeped. Will could hear his parents laugh and start to argue over who got to beep next. He ran out the front door and slid onto the back seat. His mom already had the car in gear and rolling.

"What's that rattle?" asked Will. "This car rattles."

"Extra bottles in the trunk," said Jim McCleary. "Gas money."

"Oh."

Will and Ray both sulked in the back seat as the old Ford started climbing toward Cypress Park. Will kept thinking about everything he'd been planning to do with those bottles. It didn't help that he could hear the last of the walkway rattling in the trunk.

Will breathed in the cool fresh air and listened to his mom laugh. He looked at Ray, frantically trying to keep his hair in place as wind swirled into the back seat through an open window. He didn't even realize they'd been climbing until his mom pulled over and stopped halfway up Hemlock Mountain.

"Don't want to overheat the engine," she announced. "Everyone hop out for a look."

Will and Ray didn't really want to, but they did.

"Why, I could bring my rocking chair up here and stare back the other way!" said his dad, laughing and hugging his wife.

"She parked too close to the edge for me," said Ray softly.

The city stretched out below them. It looked different and small. Will gazed up toward the top of the mountain. He couldn't see much. A thin layer of cloud surrounded the top.

"Back in the car," yelled his mom. "We're going higher."

Everyone climbed inside. The car sputtered and lurched into the mist. Will could barely see the road ahead. He leaned forward, anxious. A couple of minutes later, though, the old Ford crawled above the mist and climbed toward the summit of Hemlock Mountain. Will had seen the mountains on days like this. From the city their peaks looked like islands suspended in the sky, a fantasy land that couldn't be reached. He breathed in the cool fresh air and listened to his parents giggle almost like babies. He glanced at Ray and caught him smiling, too, staring out the window at the strange new countryside. Will closed his eyes. In his imagination he could see a little red rubber ball crashing through the roof of the Loyola theatre, climbing high above the harbour and soaring over the crest of Hemlock Mountain toward some unknown land beyond. Will's eyes sprung open.

"Mom?"

"Yeah?"

"When I'm old enough . . ."

"Yeah?"

"Teach me to drive, okay?"

Also by Ken Roberts

Crazy Ideas

Jon and Christine Anastasiou live in Sceletown, where the streets are laid out like a skeleton so that citizens can learn anatomy. They need a crazy idea to graduate from Max Barca Junior High School. That's no problem for Jon—he's crazy enough to invent the fourth most popular comic book in Canada. But Christine is having trouble. She can't seem to think of anything nutty but workable. Until one day, hanging out in Mandible Park, she sees a wrecking crew demolishing the Endicott Hotel, and her crazy idea begins to grow.

Crazy Ideas makes the improbable seem likely, the impossible believable. No one who reads this book could ever doubt that there really is an eleven-year-old genius comic book writer in the world, or that his sister, a delightfully worried impresario of destruction, is as real as the kid next door.

This irreverent book by Ken Roberts *is* crazy, and a lot of fun.